This book is dedicated to the loving memory of my daughter Yvette.

Proceeds from the sale of this book will be donated to local animal shelters.

This is a story about a girl named Yvette, her black dog named Rocky and her two cats. The black cat is named Angus and the gray cat is named Flounce.

Every night the cats sleep next to Yvette on her bed and the dog sleeps on the floor by the side of her bed. Yvette does not have any brothers or sisters and she thinks of her pets as her family.

The story begins several months before Christmas. The pets have collected all the coins and dollars that have fallen onto the floor and gotten stuck in the cushions of the sofa and chairs so that they can buy Christmas gifts for Yvette.

When Christmas is only a few weeks away, the animals wait until Yvette has left for school and her parents have gone to work.

The animals collect all the pennies, nickels, dimes, and dollars that they have found in the house. Flounce being the best at math because she sat next to Yvette in the evening while Yvette did her math homework decides she should be the one to handle the money. Rocky and Angus agree and wait as Flounce slowly counts the money and announces the total.

Rocky says to the cats, "We should go today to do our shopping for Yvette's presents." Flounce looks at him and says, "How will we get to the stores? It's been snowing the last two days and I hate to get my paws wet." Angus agrees with Flounce and says, "I hate to get my paws wet too!" Rocky tells them, "I can carry you both on my back. Just wrap up the money in a handkerchief that I can carry in my mouth." The cats agree to the plan.

Rocky unlocks the door and the cats follow him outside. Rocky closes the door. They all go down the stairs.

The animals climb on Rocky's back and they begin their shopping trip.

The first store they go to is a bookstore because they know Yvette loves to read. They enter the store and the cats jump off Rocky's back.

Each of the animals take a different aisle to look through the books. Angus sat near Yvette most often when she was learning to read and so he was the best reader and finds what he thinks is the perfect book for Yvette. Angus reads the book to Rocky and Flounce. The book is about cats and dogs, so they know it is perfect for her.

Flounce pays for the book. She counts the left-over money and tells Rocky and Angus that there is enough money left to buy another gift for Yvette.

They come to a toy store and decide it is a good place to find another gift for Yvette. They decide on three small toys. They choose a small toy black dog, small toy black cat and a small toy gray cat.

The cats climb on Rocky's back and they all return home with their gifts. When they get home, they go to the basement to wrap the gifts.

Rocky gets the wrapping paper. The cats get the ribbons. Together they wrap the gifts for Yvette and put on gift tags with their paw prints. When they finish wrapping the gifts, they hide them to wait for Christmas.

The pets are so tired from the showing trip that they fall asleep. When Yvette arrives home from school, she tries to play with the pets, but they are too sleepy. Yvette thinks this is strange, since they stay home all day.

Christmas morning comes. Yvette gives the pets their gifts.

Rocky gets a big chew bone and the cats get toys.

The pets watch as Yvette opens her gifts. While Yvette is opening the last gift, the three animals go down to the basement and bring up their gifts for Yvette and place them in front of her.

Yvette is surprised to see the gifts. When she looks at the wrappings, she sees the paw marks on the gift tags and knows the gifts are from her pets. She loves all the gifts but wonders how the pets got them for her.

Yvette is so happy with her gifts.  She hugs Rocky and he licks her face. Yvette giggles. Then she picks up Angus and hugs him. Angus begins to purr. Next, Yvette picks up Flounce and hugs her and she purrs.

Rocky, Angus and Flounce fall asleep. Yvette smiles at her sleeping pets and begin to read her new book to her new toy animals.

Now every year at Christmas time, the pets save up money and secretly go shopping for Yvette's gifts.

CPSIA information can be obtained
at www.ICGtesting.com
Printed in the USA
BVHW011517230920
589454BV00002B/70